One night,

in the middle of the night,

while everyone else was asleep,

Otilla finally ran away.

THE SKU

A Tyrolean Folktale — JON KLASSEN

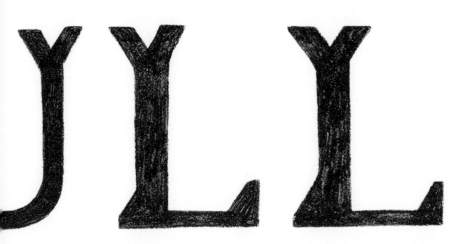

CANDLEWICK PRESS

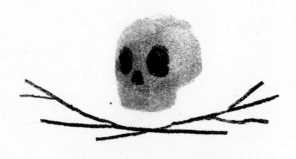

PART ONE

The Forest

The Dark

The House

Otilla ran and ran.
She ran through trees and
up hills. She ran for a long
time. All through the night.

Otilla had grown up in this forest,
but after a while the trees began
to look different. They were getting
closer together.

Otilla kept running.

As she ran, Otilla began to hear her name being called. She couldn't tell if it was someone's voice or the wind in her ears.

"Otilllllaaa."
"Otiiiiillaaaaaa."

"Otillllaaaaaaa."

"Otillll—"

Otilla suddenly tripped on a fallen branch and fell hard into the snow. She didn't get up. She could not run anymore. She listened for her name, but now it was quiet.

Otilla lay in the snow and the dark and the quiet and she cried.

When she was done crying,
she got up and began moving
forward again.

All at once, the trees stopped.
She came out of the woods and
into an open yard. In front of
her, in the distance, was a very
big, very old house.

Otilla went up to the house.
It looked abandoned, but when
she tried to open the door, it
was locked. She knocked loudly
to see if anyone was inside,
but nobody came to the door.
"Hello?" she called out.
"Hello," someone answered.

Otilla looked up to where the voice had come from. In a window above the door, she saw a skull looking at her.

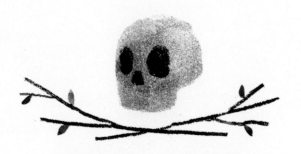

PART TWO

The Skull

The Rooms

The Dance

The skull moved himself a little
so he could see better.
"Hello," he said again.
"Hello," said Otilla. "My name
is Otilla. I ran away and I need
a place to hide and rest."

The skull was quiet for a moment.
Then he said, "I will come down
and let you in, but only if you
promise to carry me once I do.
I am just a skull, and rolling
around is difficult for me."
Otilla was quiet for a moment.
Then she said, "All right."

The skull left the window.

Otilla waited outside the door.

She waited for a long time.

It was very quiet.

Then she heard some small scratching on the other side of the door. The latch turned and the door cracked open against the snow.

The skull pushed the door
open wider.

"Thank you," said Otilla.

"You're welcome," said the skull.

Otilla picked him up. She had
never picked up a skull before.

"Come in," said the skull.

"I will show you the house."

"All right," said Otilla.

They walked into the hall.

"It is a nice house," said Otilla.

"Yes," said the skull. "I have always liked it here."

"Have you lived here for a long time?" said Otilla.

"Yes," said the skull.

They went into a room.
"This is the fireplace room," said
the skull. "I come here to drink
tea by the fire in the evenings."
"You can make tea?" said Otilla.
"No, not anymore," said the skull.

"Can you make a fire?" said Otilla.

"No," said the skull.

They were quiet.

"Is that you in the picture?"
said Otilla.

"It used to be," said the skull.

They went into the garden room.

"Oh, I like this room," said Otilla.

"This is my favorite room," said
the skull.

"Can you eat the pears?" said Otilla.

"I can eat the ones that fall on the
ground, but I can't reach the good
ones on the branches," said the skull.

"I will get one for you," said Otilla.
She held a pear for him and he took
a bite. The bite of pear went through
him and fell onto the floor.

"Ah, delicious," said the skull.

"Thank you."

They went into a room with
masks hung on the walls.
"What are these masks for?" said Otilla.
"I used to collect them," said the skull.
"Can you wear them?" said Otilla.
"They are just for show," said the skull.
"You are not supposed to wear them."

They went downstairs.

"What is this room?" said Otilla.

"This is the dungeon," said the skull.

"There is nobody in it now."

"What is this hole?" said Otilla.

"That is a bottomless pit," said the skull.

Otilla threw the core of her pear
into the hole and listened. It did
not make a sound.
"Do you want to see the tower?"
said the skull.
"All right," said Otilla.

They climbed the steps up the tower.

"Does anyone else know about this house?" said Otilla.

"No," said the skull. "You are the first person to find it in a very long time."

They got to the top and walked out onto the balcony.

"You can see everything from here," said the skull.

"It's beautiful," said Otilla.

"Careful," said the skull. "The wall is not very high and it is a long way down if you fall."

They looked out over the forest.

"You said you ran away," said
the skull.

"Yes," said Otilla.

"You don't want them to find you."

"No," said Otilla. "I don't."

The skull waited to see if she wanted
to say any more, but she didn't.
"All right," said the skull.
Then he said, "There is a big room
I haven't shown you."
"How big?" said Otilla.

"This is the biggest room I have
  ever seen," said Otilla.
"This is the ballroom," said the skull.
"It was for dancing. There were lots
  of dances here."
"I went to a dance once," said Otilla.
"But it was not in a room like this.
  I did like the dancing, though."
"I love dancing," said the skull.

Otilla put her mask back on. She carried the skull to the middle of the ballroom. She held him to face her.

"Would you care to dance, sir?"
said Otilla.
"M'lady," said the skull.

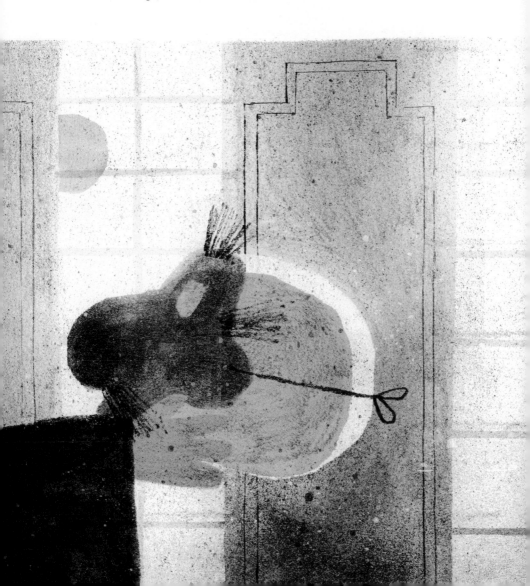

They danced
and danced
and danced
until it got dark.

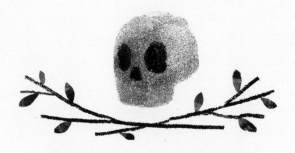

PART THREE

The Secret

The Bedroom

The Headless Skeleton

When it was dark, Otilla made some
tea and a fire in the fireplace room.
"Would you give me some tea,
please?" said the skull.
Otilla took a teacup and poured the
tea through his mouth and onto
the chair.
"Ah, nice and warm," said the skull.
"Thank you."

"You can spend the night here,
 if you want to," said the skull.
"I do want to," said Otilla.
"There is something I should tell
 you," said the skull.
 Otilla put her tea down.
"There is a skeleton that comes

here, to this house," said the skull. "It is a headless skeleton. It walks around the halls looking for me. When it finds me, it chases me."

"Has it ever caught you?" said Otilla.

"No," said the skull quietly. "But I am not as fast as I used to be."

Otilla looked closely at the skull.

"You don't want it to catch you."

"No," whispered the skull. "I don't."

"Will it come tonight?" said Otilla.

The skull looked at the fire.

"It comes every night," he said.

Otilla looked at the fire too.

"All right," she said.

She kept looking at the fire, and

she started to think.

When it was time to go to sleep, the skull showed Otilla to a bedroom. It was a nice room. There was a big comfortable bed and some pajamas for her to wear. Otilla liked the pajamas.

"We should try to get some sleep,"
said the skull. "The skeleton will
come soon enough."

Otilla blew out the light.

They slept deeply and peacefully for
a long time.

The house was dark and very quiet.
Until, in the middle of the night . . .

a headless skeleton opened the
bedroom door. From somewhere
in the skeleton's chest came a voice,
but it only shouted one thing:

"GIVE ME THAT SKULL.
I WANT THAT SKULL."

The skeleton ran into the room.
It was faster than Otilla had
expected. She had just enough
time to grab the skull before it
reached him. The skeleton pulled
at the skull, trying to get him
away from her, but Otilla held
on tight. She did not let go.

Finally she got the skull free.
She slipped past the skeleton
and ran for the door.

"GIVE ME THAT SKULL."

"I WANT THAT SKULL."

"GIVE ME THAT SKULL."

"I WANT THAT SKULL."

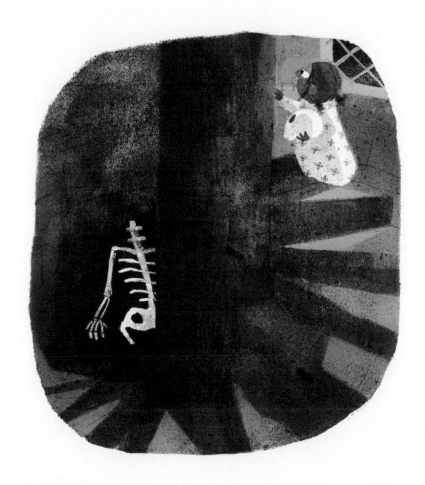

"GIVE ME THAT SKULL."

"I WANT THAT—"

They watched the skeleton fall into the dark until they heard it land, the sound of bones hitting the ground. They listened some more, but they did not hear anything after that.

"All right," said Otilla. "Time for bed."

Otilla carried the skull quietly
back down to the bedroom. She
put him on the pillow and tucked
him under the blanket. Then she
put on her coat.

"Aren't you going to sleep too?"
said the skull.

"In a little while," said Otilla,
patting the skull gently. "I'll be
back soon."

She blew out the light and closed
the bedroom door.

PART FOUR

The Bones

The Fire

The Pit

Otilla went to the kitchen and found a bucket, a kettle with tea leaves, a teacup, and a rolling pin.

Then she went out into the night and climbed down, slowly and carefully, to where the skeleton had fallen.

When she got to the bottom,
she found the skeleton's bones
scattered everywhere.

She gathered them into the bucket.
She found every single one.

Otilla carried the bucket of bones to a rock. She took a bone out of the bucket and put it on the rock. Then she took out the rolling pin, held it over her head, and smashed the bone. She smashed it over and over, into smaller and smaller pieces, until the pieces were as small as they could get. Then she took out another bone and she did it again. She did it to all of them.

Then Otilla made a fire. She made it huge and hot. She melted some snow in the kettle with the tea leaves and made tea over the fire.

Then she took the bone pieces and threw them into the flames. She poured her tea into the teacup and drank it as she watched the pieces burn to ash.

When the fire was over, she gathered the ashes into the bucket and carried it back up the hill, back to the house. She went down to the dungeon and dropped the whole bucket into the bottomless pit. She watched it fall into the dark and listened. It did not make a sound.

Then she climbed back upstairs and went to bed.

PART FIVE

Breakfast

In the morning Otilla and the skull had breakfast. Otilla made tea and picked some pears from the branches.

"I'm sorry last night was so frightening," said the skull.

Otilla smiled and patted the skull.

"It's over now," she said.

"Thank you for helping me," said the skull.

"You're welcome," said Otilla.

"I wonder if the skeleton will ever come back," said the skull.
Otilla cut a piece of pear.
"It won't," she said.

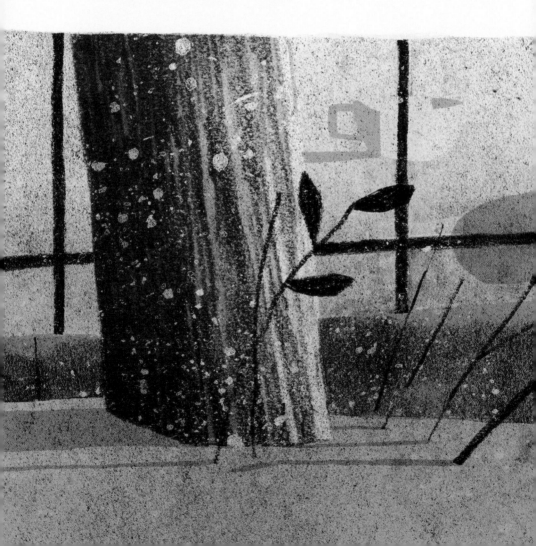

The skull looked out the window.
"It's a nice day outside," he said.
"Do you want to go for a walk?"

They went for a walk.

It was a nice day outside.

Otilla stopped and gave the skull
a bite of pear. It went through him
and fell onto the sled.

"Thank you," said the skull. He took
another bite.

"You know," he said, chewing the
pear, "you could stay here with
me, if you want."

"Do you want me to stay?"
said Otilla.

"Yes," said the skull.
"I do."

"All right," said Otilla.

THE

END

AUTHOR'S NOTE

I found this story in a library in Alaska. I was there to do a presentation at the library, and I was looking at books on the shelf before it started. I picked out a book of folktales and looked at the table of contents and saw a story called "The Skull" and thought that was a good title. I stood there and read it, put the book back on the shelf, did my presentation, and left the library.

I thought about the story on the plane back home, and then again when I got home, and then I thought about it every now and then for about a year. Finally, I thought, I should probably read that story again. I couldn't remember the name of the book it had been in, so I wrote to the library in Alaska and told them about the skull story and somehow they found the book and sent me the name. Librarians are really good at that.

But when I sat down and read the story again, I was surprised. It wasn't the story I remembered. In the year in between, my brain had changed it without telling me. In the Alaska book, Otilla bests the headless skeleton simply by not letting go of the skull all night while he tries to pull it away, and, at dawn, as the sun comes through the window, the spell over all of them is broken. The skeleton vanishes and the skull turns into a beautiful lady in white. The castle is filled with nice things and children to play with, and the lady in white gives all of this to Otilla and then she also vanishes. I didn't remember any of that. My brain had changed the ending a lot. It had changed it, more or less, to the ending in the book you are holding. I liked my brain's new version.

This is a very interesting thing that our brains do to stories. If you read this book once and put it back on the shelf, and a year from now someone asks you how this story went, the same thing will happen: your brain will change it. You will tell them a story that is a little different, maybe in a way your brain likes better. I like folktales because that is what is supposed to happen to them. They are supposed to be changed by who is telling them, and you never find them the same way twice. I hope that you liked my brain's version.

For Isaac

The original retelling of this tale was found in *A Book of Ghosts and Goblins*, written by Ruth Manning-Sanders and illustrated by Robin Jacques (New York: Dutton, 1969).

The traditional Tyrolean carved masks on page 33 are inspired by those found in the book *Perchtenmasken in Österreich* [Carved custom masks of the Austrian Alps] by Leopold Schmidt (Vienna, Austria: Hermann Böhlaus Nachfolger, 1972).

First edition 2023

Library of Congress Catalog Card Number 2022936945
ISBN 978-1-5362-2336-1

23 24 25 26 27 28 APS 10 9 8 7 6 5 4 3 2 1

Printed in Humen, Dongguan, China

This book was typeset in New Century Schoolbook.
The illustrations were done in graphite and ink and finished digitally.

Candlewick Press
99 Dover Street
Somerville, Massachusetts 02144

www.candlewick.com